PUFFIN BOOKS

THE SPOOKY WORLD OF COSMO JONES
GHOST TRAIN

Daniel Postgate lives in Whitstable, Kent. He has worked as a newspaper cartoonist for many years and more recently has written and illustrated a number of children's books. He likes swimming, walking, cooking and watching the telly.

D0508131

Another book by Daniel Postgate

SUPER MOLLY AND THE
LOLLY RESCUE

Daniel Postgate
The Spooky World of Cosmo Jones
Ghost Train

PUFFIN BOOKS

For Leo

PUFFIN BOOKS

Published by the Penguin Group
Penguin Books Ltd, 27 Wrights Lane, London W8 5TZ, England
Penguin Putnam Inc., 375 Hudson Street, New York, New York 10014, USA
Penguin Books Australia Ltd, Ringwood, Victoria, Australia
Penguin Books Canada Ltd, 10 Alcorn Avenue, Toronto, Ontario, Canada M4V 3B2
Penguin Books (NZ) Ltd, Private Bag 102902, NSMC, Auckland, New Zealand

On the World Wide Web at: www.penguin.com

Penguin Books Ltd, Registered Offices: Harmondsworth, Middlesex, England

First published 2000
1 3 5 7 9 10 8 6 4 2

Printed in Hong Kong by Midas Printing Ltd

British Library Cataloguing in Publication Data
A CIP catalogue record for this book is available from the British Library

ISBN 0-141-30684-X

Contents

1. Cosmo

Cosmo Jones loved anything to do with ghosts and monsters and things from other planets. His bedroom was stacked high with books and comics all about that sort of thing.

Most evenings, when other kids were out rollerblading or playing football, Cosmo was tucked away

in his
bedroom,
reading about
headless ghosts, strange chicken
people from Venus, or something
else just as weird.

One afternoon, Cosmo was up in
his bedroom thinking how great it
would be if ghosts and aliens really
did exist. This was his favourite

daydream, and just as he was
getting to the bit where he actually
meets one of these strange creatures,
his mother shouted up the stairs,
"Cosmo, time for your tea!"

While Cosmo was chewing
his beans on toast and idly
flicking through the local paper,

he spotted an advertisement that thrilled him to the bone. This is what it said:

THE PRICKLEBOURNE GHOST HUNTERS' SOCIETY

A new society interested in all things "spooky" is keen to find members. All those interested please come to the Cuthbert Road car park on Wednesday 28 July, at 6.30 p.m. prompt. Dress casual.

Cosmo could hardly wait.

2. At the Car Park

At six thirty on Wednesday 28 July, Cosmo arrived at Cuthbert Road car park only to find it completely empty. Feeling rather disappointed, he decided the advertisement must have been some sort of prank. He was just about to turn on his heels and head home when he heard someone shout, "Cosmo!"

He spotted a head sticking out of the window of a shed at the far end of the car park.

"What are you doing here?" it said.

Cosmo jogged nearer to the shed until he saw that the head belonged to Mr Pringle, the car park attendant and an old friend of the family.

"Oh … I'm just here for some silly meeting, Mr Pringle," he said.

"Really?" replied Mr Pringle. "Funnily enough, I'm expecting visitors too. Enthusiasts of all things strange and unknown, as it happens."

"Ah," said Cosmo. "Then you're a member of the Pricklebourne Ghost Hunters' Society?"

"Yes, yes!" exclaimed Mr Pringle.

"Then ... I think I've come to see you, Mr Pringle," said Cosmo.

"Oh good," said Mr Pringle with a grin. "Come in, we'll start the meeting." And he disappeared back into the shed.

When Cosmo entered the shed he noticed that he was the only person there, apart from Mr Pringle, of course, who had kindly unfolded a chair for him.

"Is anyone else coming?" asked Cosmo.

Mr Pringle slapped his hand to his forehead and thought for a second. "No," he said, finally.

"Oh," said Cosmo.

"Never mind," chirped Mr Pringle, clapping his hands together. "I declare the first meeting of the Pricklebourne Ghost Hunters' Society officially OPEN!" He got out a clipboard and sat himself down.

"Let's start by finding out what sort of unusual experiences our members have had."

"Well, to be honest, I haven't had any," said Cosmo.

"AH-HA!" said Mr Pringle, and he scribbled something on his clipboard.

"How about you?" Cosmo asked.

Mr Pringle put his clipboard on his lap and spread his hands over it. "Just the other night I was reading a book about ghosts when I began to feel sleepy. I put the book on the dining table and went to bed. And in the morning the book HAD GONE." Then he crossed his arms and raised his eyebrows at Cosmo.

"Perhaps Mrs Pringle tidied it

away?" suggested Cosmo.

"Perhaps ... perhaps," mumbled
Mr Pringle, then he squinted at his
clipboard. "Now, what's next? ...
Ah yes!" He pulled a mobile phone
from his pocket and held it up.

"Modern technology," he
announced. "I have put a card in
the window of Mr Patel's shop. If

anyone finds themselves troubled by ghosts or even aliens, they can take my number and contact me twenty-four hours a day!"

Cosmo shuffled uncomfortably in his seat. "Erm, Mr Pringle, I really like this new society of yours, but I'm not sure it's quite what I had in –"

BEEP BEEP!

Cosmo and Mr Pringle both
looked at the phone. It was beeping.
Mr Pringle switched it on and
cautiously held it to his ear.

"Hello? Yes, I am he. Yes,
yes ..." Mr Pringle glanced up at
Cosmo, his face was flushed with
excitement. "We'll be over right
away." He put away the phone,

jumped to his feet and slapped a
hand on Cosmo's shoulder.

"Ghosts reported at the Webster
household, forty-three Gladstone
Road ... Cosmo, THIS IS IT."

3. At the Websters'

"Here we are," said Mr Pringle when they arrived at the Websters' house. "Now, Cosmo, don't forget to act professional. We don't want them to think we don't know what we're doing." Then he rang the doorbell.

The door opened just a little bit and a man's face appeared.

"Mr Webster?" said Mr Pringle. "We're from the P.G.H.S."

"The what?" said Mr Webster.

"The Pricklebourne Ghost Hunters' Society," said Mr Pringle. "You phoned about ghosts."

"That must have been my wife," said Mr Webster, and he opened the door

to let them in.

In the living room, Mr Webster turned off the television. "Erm … ghosts. Yes, it's been horrible. Gran's not herself, the twins are noisier than ever and the parrot's right off his nuts. Don't believe in ghosts myself, of course."

Mr Pringle took out his clipboard and licked the end of his pencil. "So what sort of things have you seen then?" he asked.

"Erm," said Mr Webster, scratching his head, "screaming hags, howling goblins. Er, huge wailing ghosts. Erm, skeletons …"

"And this hasn't changed your mind about ghosts in any way?" asked Mr Pringle.

"Certainly not," replied Mr Webster. "I've never believed in that sort of thing and I'm blowed if I'm about to start now."

"You can never be too sure though," said Mrs Webster, coming in with a tray of tea and biscuits.

"Ah, good evening, Mrs Webster," said Mr Pringle."Tea and biscuits, oh lovely."

"I heard you come in, so I thought I'd make a brew, and there's some nice ginger cake for the young lad –" Mrs Webster stopped speaking and stared down at the tray. The cups had started rattling about on it.

Cosmo noticed that the room had suddenly become dark and very cold.

"TAKE COVER!" Mrs Webster suddenly screamed. She threw the tray in the air, belly-flopped on to the carpet and wriggled under the coffee table.

Mr Webster tutted, eased himself on to the sofa and shook open a copy of the *Pricklebourne Gazette*.

A china pig jiggled across the top of the television as a deep growling sound filled the room. The sound quickly grew into a deafening roar.

"Shouldn't we hide, Mr Pringle?" yelled Cosmo, pulling at his sleeve.

"Oh, no, no, no!" hollered Mr Pringle. "Lesson one for every ghost hunter, always stand your ground!"

Suddenly, a bright white light burst through the wall.

That was enough
for Cosmo. He jumped, and
tumbled behind a chair. Peeping out
from behind it, he saw a trainload
of horrible ghosts fly into the room,
shrieking and waving their bony
arms about.

They flew straight through
Mr Pringle, rustling the pages of
Mr Webster's newspaper, then flew
through another wall and off
around the house. Finally, the
shrieking faded away and the
room became quiet and still again.

Mr Pringle stood, clipboard in
hand, frozen to the spot. His face
was a ghostly white with a tinge of
blue.

4. Ghost Train

"Oooh, that gave me a bit of a fright," said Grandma Webster, shuffling in through the door. "What's the matter with him?" she asked, pointing at Mr Pringle, who was being helped out of the living room by Cosmo and Mrs Webster.

"He's had a nasty shock, Gran.

I think we'll pop him on your bed
for a bit." And they led Mr Pringle
up the corridor to Grandma
Webster's room.

Mr Pringle lay on Grandma
Webster's bed, shivering. "C-Cosmo,
they were ghosts, *real* ghosts," he
whispered, grasping Cosmo's arm.

"I know, Mr Pringle, isn't it exciting?" said Cosmo.

"I think I'll stay here on the bed for a while. I feel a bit … funny," whimpered Mr Pringle. "Cosmo, it's up to you now – investigate, find out what you can … for me, for the Society." Then he reared up. "And for the sake of all that is good in the world, HELP THESE POOR PEOPLE!" Then he fell back on to the bed, exhausted.

"Well, I'll do my best," said Cosmo, and he marched out of the bedroom.

He entered the living room to find the Websters' twin boys jumping up and down on the sofa.

"Scary chuff-chuff!" they yelled.

"Sorry to hear about the other

bloke," sighed Mr Webster, folding up his newspaper. "Last time we had trouble like this, the telly went completely dead, right in the middle of the football. Very annoying."

"I'll bet," said Cosmo.

"So what's causing this?" asked Mr Webster. "The plumbing, the central heating, unusual weather?"

"Come on, Frank," said Mrs Webster. "Don't be so stubborn, you know it *must* be ghosts."

"Yes," said Cosmo. "You've definitely got ghosts. I've read about a case like this in a story called *The Curse of the Chipmunk's Claw*. I think I can help, but I'll need something that swings, like a watch on a chain."

"We've got something!" yelled the twins, and they ran off to get it.

"Does a chipmunk have a claw?" asked Mr Webster.

"It doesn't matter," replied Cosmo. "What's important is what happened in the story. These people were being haunted by some horrible ghosts, OK? And it turned out that one of them was sort of *attracting* the ghosts, but didn't realize it."

"No!" said Mrs Webster.

"Yes," said Cosmo. "They hypnotized everyone to find out who this person was."

The Webster twins came back with a large plastic toy of a man with a big happy face who was wearing a large stripy tie. "It's Funny Man!" they yelled. "Look!" They wound a key in the back of Funny Man and set him on the table. His tie began to swing from side to side like a pendulum, while his eyes looked this way then that.

"Well, it'll have to do," said Cosmo. "Now I want you all to sit down, empty your minds and stare at Funny Man. Just watch his tie swing. Hopefully, we'll find out who the 'ghost-magnet' is."

"You're joking," said Mr Webster.

"Well," said Cosmo, "let's give it a try anyway."

Everyone did as they were told and, after a minute, Mrs Webster waved a finger at Grandma Webster. "Look," she whispered.

Grandma's eyes were fluttering, her lips were twitching and her nostrils started to flare. Suddenly her head fell back and she let out a long growling snort.

"Grandma Webster, what do you see?" asked Cosmo.

Grandma sat bolt upright and blinked. "Oh, sorry," she said, "I must have dropped off."

"Oh, this is ridiculous!" exclaimed Mr Webster, jumping up from his chair.

"FUNFAIR!" croaked the
Websters' parrot.

Everyone gasped. "He's never
said *that* before!" said Mrs Webster.

They all crowded round the cage.
The parrot had a strange, faraway
look in his eyes.

"Big dipper, merry-go-round, helter-skelter, big wheel. Squawk!" he squawked.

"A funfair?!" exclaimed Mr Webster.

"Parrot, tell us more!" said Cosmo excitedly.

"Ghosts, GHOSTS, GHOSTS!" he shrieked, shaking his feathers. "GHOST TRAIN! Roll up, roll up, scare the Websters. Make 'em shake, make 'em shiver. See Grandma's teeth rattle, see Mrs Webster quiver, see the parrot jump about in his cage. Ha ha ha! All the fun of the fair."

"AH-HA!" exclaimed Cosmo, making everyone jump. "That's it!"

"What's what?!" exclaimed Mr Webster.

"I read about something like this in a story called *The Phantom Fun Park*," said Cosmo in a whisper. "Your house is being used as a ghost-train ride. But instead of you going on the ghost train to be scared, the ghosts go on it to scare *you.*"

"No!" gasped Mrs Webster. "So we're nothing but a fairground attraction ... Those *cheeky rascals.* What can we do?"

"I've got an idea," said Cosmo. "Some ghost hunters believe that although ghosts are quite scary, they are also big cowards. They jump out in front of you and go BOO or whatever, then they disappear ... in other words, they *run away.* I mean, how cowardly can you get?"

"True," said Mrs Webster thoughtfully.

"So," Cosmo grinned and rubbed his hands together, "let's give them a taste of their own medicine!"

5. The Websters Strike Back

The Websters pulled a trunk down from the attic and tipped out a pile of fancy-dress costumes.

"Right, choose who you want to be and remember, the scarier the better," said Cosmo. "I'm going to be a vampire."

"But *I* wanted to be a vampire," moaned Mr Webster.

"Never mind, darling, you can be a werewolf," said Mrs Webster. "You're so hairy, you're halfway there already!"

The Webster twins put on their Halloween costumes. Mrs Webster dressed up as a witch and Cosmo borrowed some plastic fangs and a cloak. He made a very good vampire. Grandma found some old

chains to rattle, cut two eye-holes in a sheet and threw it over herself. Mr Webster climbed into a gorilla suit, painted his face white and put on a green fright wig. He didn't look like a werewolf, but he looked pretty scary all the same.

Just as they had all got ready, the room turned dark and they heard a low growl.

Cosmo put in his fangs and threw up his hands. "OK, everybody, take your positions. It's SHOW TIME!"

The ghost train burst through the wall again, but this time it screeched to a halt and its ghostly passengers all stared open-mouthed at Cosmo and the Websters shrieking and yelling and leaping

about the lounge in their gruesome
costumes. Grandma was
particularly good. She swung the
chains around her head and wailed
like a foghorn. The ghosts screamed
in horror, the train swivelled round
and shot back through the wall,

leaving a blast of cold air behind it.

"We did it!" yelled the Websters, and they danced about singing, "We are the champions".

"Well, let's hope that's the end of that," sighed Cosmo.

But unfortunately, it wasn't.

There was a sudden cloud of smoke, followed by a nasty smell of rotting cabbages, and there stood a horrible great ... THING. Its eyes flashed hot and white, and smoke billowed from its ears.

"Who's spoiled my fun?" it boomed.

6. Nonsense

"What do we do?" cried Mrs Webster.

"RUN!" yelled Cosmo.

There was a scramble for the door. The Websters tumbled into the hall and dashed up the corridor. Grandma and Mr Webster jostled neck-and-neck for the lead, closely followed by the twins and

Mrs Webster, while
Cosmo trailed last. The
leaders rushed through Grandma's
bedroom door, trampled over a
rather surprised Mr Pringle, and
piled into the bedroom cupboard.
Cosmo grabbed Mr Pringle,

dragged him off the
bed and into the cupboard, and
pulled the door shut.

Outside they heard the clomp,
clomp, clomp of heavy feet in the
corridor.

"Ow!" yelled Mr Webster.

"Someone's got their elbow in my face."

"Well, you're treading all over my foot, you clumsy great ape!" snapped Grandma Webster.

Somebody started to whimper. It was Mr Pringle.

"Do be quiet," hissed Mrs Webster. "We don't want that thing finding our hiding place."

But by this time, the thing *had* found their hiding place and was waiting for them to stop bickering.

"SHUT UP," it finally roared, making the cupboard rattle and its inhabitants fall silent. "You have meddled with matters you don't understand. And for that you must PAY!" Then it snarled and beat its giant fists against the walls. "I'll frazzle you to a crisp, I'll pulverize you to a pulp, I'll mash you to a … to a …"

"Mush?" suggested Grandma Webster.

"Yes!" yelled the thing. Then it laughed hideously and roared some more.

"Oh, I've had enough of this," said Mr Webster. "I'm going out there."

"Frank, you must be mad," hissed Mrs Webster. "That thing will tear you limb from limb."

"Nonsense, Maureen," said Mr Webster. He pushed open the cupboard door and stepped out.

"Sticks and stones can break my bones, but words can never hurt me," he sang.

"WHAT?" bellowed the thing.

Its eyes grew as wide as saucers and smoke hissed from between its teeth.

"I'm not scared of you, because you don't really exist," explained Mr Webster.

"How dare you!" hissed the thing. "I *do* exist!"

"Then I'm afraid we'll have to agree to disagree, OK?" said Mr Webster.

"I DO EXIST, I DO, I DO!" insisted the thing, then it let out a howl that shook the whole house.

"I'm sorry, I can't hear you," said Mr Webster. Then he crossed his arms and started looking around and whistling.

The thing's lips quivered and a sudden look of doubt filled its eyes.

"AAAAAAAAAAAAArgh," it cried. Throwing up its great arms, it burst into a huge ball of glaring white light, then disappeared completely.

Everyone in the cupboard stared out, absolutely amazed.

"Told you," said Mr Webster, brushing his hands together. "It's all a load of nonsense." Then he turned to the cupboard. "Right, you lot, I'm off down the pub."

And with that, he strode down the corridor and out through the front door.

Everyone, except Mr Pringle, who was still feeling a bit funny, jostled their way to the front window and watched him march off down the road.

"Have you ever known anyone so *stubborn*?" said Mrs Webster. "What a hero."

"Shouldn't we tell him that he's still got a gorilla suit and green wig on?" asked Cosmo.

"Oh no," replied Mrs Webster. "I'm sure he'll find out soon enough."

7. At the Car Park Again

Back in the shed at the Cuthbert Road car park, a recovered Mr Pringle made some final notes on his clipboard. "I'm just jotting down that the first meeting of the Pricklebourne Ghost Hunters' Society has been surprisingly successful," he said, beaming at Cosmo. "Thanks to you, and Mr

Webster of course." Then he looked a little embarrassed. "Obviously, I'm not really any good at face-to-face combat with the unknown. In future, this will remain our headquarters and I'll run things from here, while *you* will be our man of action. How does that sound?"

"OK," said Cosmo.

"And don't you worry," Mr Pringle continued, "I'm still right there with you, it's just that I won't be – er ... right there with you, if you see what I mean. And finally, I think we should no longer be called the Pricklebourne Ghost Hunters' Society. Instead we'll be called the Pricklebourne League of

Paranormal Investigation. The P.L.O.P.I."

"Ploppy," said Cosmo.

"Yes," said Mr Pringle. "I declare this meeting at a close." He got up and ruffled Cosmo's hair. "You did good, kid," he said.

Cosmo made his way across the car park. *You did good, kid!* he thought.

Mr Pringle watches too much American telly. He'd just got to the edge of the car park when he heard his name called.

"Cosmo!" yelled Mr Pringle through the open window. "I've got a Mrs Wentworth of five Gorral Road on the phone.

Apparently she's got werewolves in her garden and they're digging up the shrubbery."

"Right you are, Mr Pringle!" yelled Cosmo and off he ran to investigate.